THE SOCK THIEF

Ana Crespo

pictures by
Nana Gonzalez

ALBERT WHITMAN & COMPANY
CHICAGO, ILLINOIS

Para meu pai e para meu tio Franzé.
Amo vocês!—AC

Para Teresa y Alberto por dejarme ser.
Para Fede y Lauren por llenar mi
vida de amor y alegría—NG

Library of Congress Cataloging-in-Publication
data is on file with the publisher.

Text copyright © 2015 Ana Crespo
Pictures copyright © 2015 Albert Whitman & Company
Pictures by Nana Gonzalez
Published in 2015 by Albert Whitman & Company
ISBN 978-0-8075-7538-3

Printed in China.
10 9 8 7 6 5 4 3 2 1 HH 18 17 16 15 14

Design by Jordan Kost

For more information about Albert Whitman & Company,
visit our web site at www.albertwhitman.com.

In a small Brazilian town, Felipe
leaves home earlier than usual.
He walks a long way to school.

Still sleepy, he stops by his family's mango tree. He picks the pinkest mangoes he sees. The sweet fruit wakes him up.

Felipe has a secret. Once a week, he needs socks. He would use his own socks if he had any, but he doesn't. Why own socks if the only shoes he owns is a pair of worn-out flip-flops?

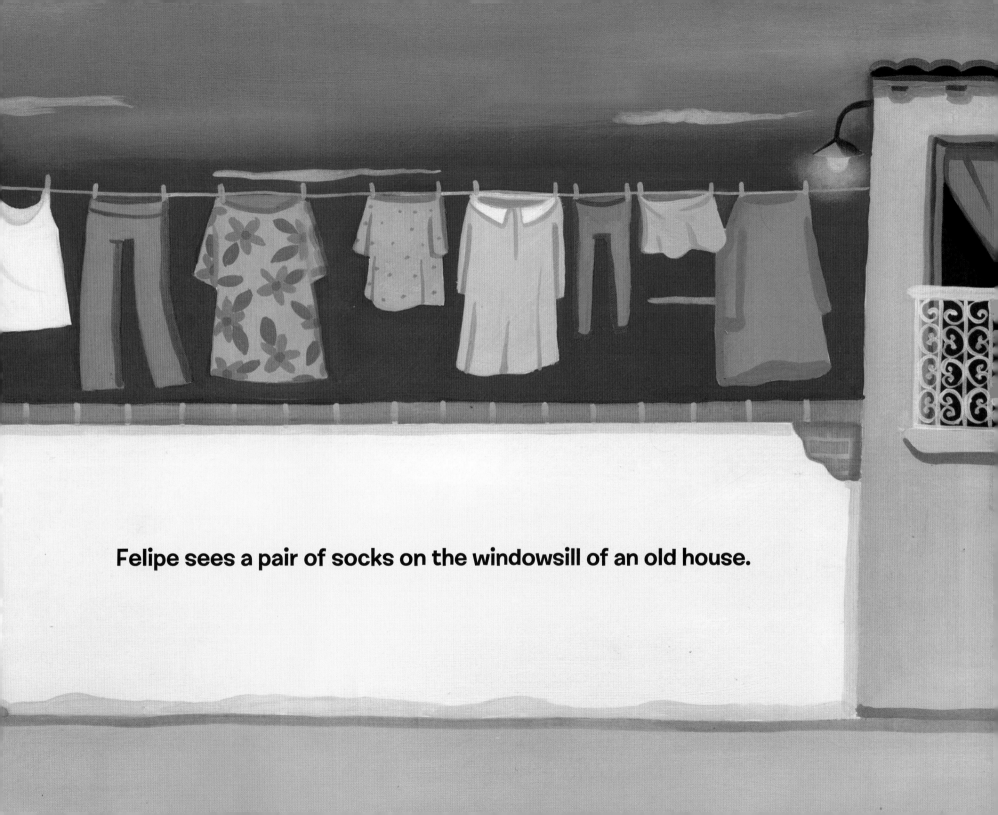

Felipe sees a pair of socks on the windowsill of an old house.

He seizes the socks and leaves a mango on the front steps.

And he wakes up a dog.

"Au, au, au!" the dog woofs in Portuguese.

Felipe runs away as fast as he can.

Panting, Felipe stops running, pulls an old newspaper from his bag, and starts working.

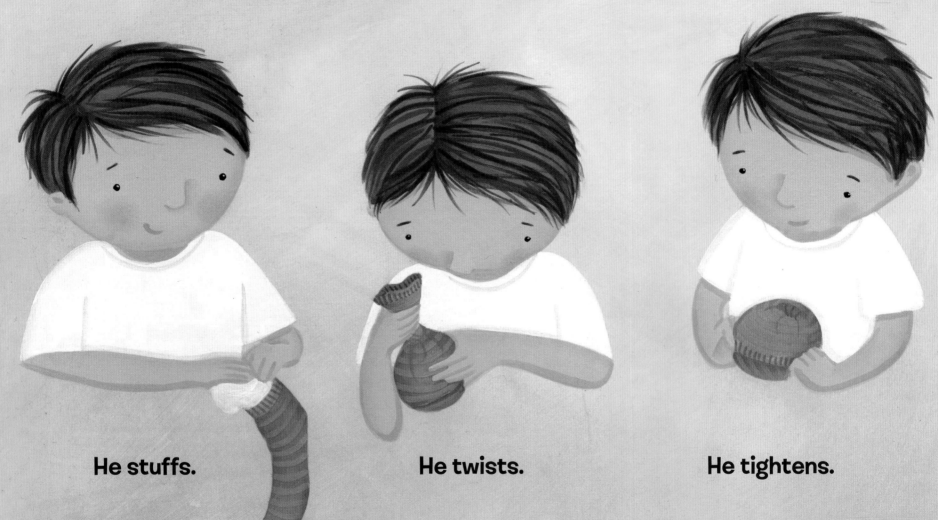

He stuffs.

He twists.

He tightens.

He stuffs, twists, and tightens again.

Soon Felipe is searching for more socks. There is a pair hanging from a clothesline. He snatches the socks and leaves a mango.

Then a rooster threatens to tell his secret to the entire neighborhood.

"Cocoricó!" it screams in Portuguese.

Again Felipe is on the run.

He stops only when the rooster is far behind him and the cocoricó is just a whisper. He stuffs, twists, and tightens once, then twice. Three times, four times.

As Felipe gets closer to his school,

he is not sure he will get all the socks he needs.

But just when he thinks there are no more socks to be found, Felipe spies some! This pair of very large socks rests on a fence, next to a parrot. Felipe swipes the socks and leaves a mango.

He is safe until a loud voice behind him says,

"Obrigado,
      obrigado,
            obrigado!"

The parrot is thanking him, very loudly, in Portuguese. And once again, Felipe runs away.

Felipe stuffs, twists, and tightens once and twice.
He gives it a few stitches.

Finally he is ready for school.

At the sight of Felipe, his friends run to him and ask,
"Did you bring the soccer ball?"

"Here it is," Felipe answers.

They play soccer before school.

They play soccer during recess.

They play soccer after school.

The newspaper-stuffed sock ball survives the muddy field and every hard hit. It survives defenses, disputes, and goals.

It even survives the puppy
that wants to play too.

After school, on his long journey back home, Felipe returns each pair of socks. Next to them, he leaves a note.

"Obrigado pelas meias!" *Thank you for the socks!* He hopes the owners of the socks don't mind that he borrowed them for the day.

OBRIGADO PELAS MEIAS!

But what Felipe doesn't realize is that everyone knows his secret and everyone is happy to help—and to eat the mangoes.

AUTHOR'S NOTE

As a young girl, I never got tired of hearing my father's childhood stories. One of the stories that fascinated me the most was about playing soccer with newspaper-stuffed socks or, in his case, newspaper-stuffed stockings. When my father was growing up in Rio de Janeiro, Brazil, in the late 1950s, soccer balls were extremely expensive, especially for a family of seven. So kids had to be creative.

My father and uncle would take my grandma's stockings and do exactly what Felipe does in the story—stuffs, twists, and tightens, again, again, and again. The ball they made was soft and approximately five inches in diameter. They spent several afternoons in the backyard kicking the ball back and forth or on the city streets playing soccer with their friends.

However, newspaper-stuffed sock balls were not a creation of my family. Many children in Brazil played soccer with them. The most famous example is probably Pelé, who used them as a child in the 1940s. Pelé grew up to win three World Cups as part of the Brazilian National Team in 1958, 1962, and 1970. Even today, he is considered by many as the best soccer player the world has ever seen.

PORTUGUESE GLOSSARY

Here are some Portuguese words you can learn and practice with your friends!

dog – cachorro

mango – manga

rooster – galo

soccer – futebol

socks – meias

friends – amigos

parrot – papagaio

school – escola

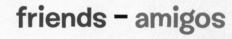

soccer ball – bola de futebol

thank you – obrigado